This book is dedicated with love and gratitude to
Meg, Annalisa, Genevieve and Naomi,
and to my beloved mother, Ruth Keech.

With special thanks to:
Mick Moore and Landy
Fee, Charlie and the boys

www.veronicalamond.com

Under licence from Jaguar Land Rover
This book is not a representation of Jaguar Land Rover or product performance

Landy

Written and illustrated by
Veronica Lamond

Landy stood at the bottom of the field.
His engine wouldn't start and his tyres were flat.

He felt very sad.

James, the farmer, raced past in his new red pick-up.

"Don't be sad, Landy," said the ducks.
"We like to sit on your roof and
dry our wings in the sunshine."

"Don't be sad, Landy," said the sheep.
"We love to huddle up next to
you when it's cold and windy."

Landy sighed and said, "When James was a little boy, I used to help his dad with all the jobs on the farm."

"We mowed the fields, we sawed the wood

and, in the winter, we carried hay to the animals."

Jack lived near the farm.
One day he was out walking
with Molly, his dog.

He was excited to find Landy.
"I wonder if the farmer will let
me take you home!" he said

Jack and Molly ran up to the
farmyard.

"It'll take a lot of work to get Landy going again," said James. "But you can have a go."

He drove Tractor down across the fields. "I'll come back to see you all!" Landy called to the animals.

Tractor rumbled off down the road to Jack's house.

Jack got out his tools, opened Landy's bonnet and set to work.

Then, at last…

he was just like new!

"Come on, Landy," said Jack. "Let's go and say hello to James and the animals."

They hadn't gone far before Landy suddenly stopped.
Molly fell THUD! onto the floor.

There were lambs on the road, skipping about.
"BEEP! BEEP!" said Landy.
Jack jumped out and bundled them into the back.
"BAAA!"

Further along a calf cried, "MOOOoo!"
She was stuck in a ditch. Jack heaved her out
and put her in with the lambs.

"EEK! EEK! EEK!" Some piglets were running through the wheat. Jack and Molly chased them and caught them.

"In you all go," laughed Jack.

"WOOF! WOOF!" barked Molly, just so they all knew who was in charge.

Landy felt very proud as he drove everyone
up the bumpy track.
"BEEP! BEEP!" he said as they
turned into the farmyard.

The cow licked her muddy, wet calf.

The sheep lay down with her tired little lambs

and the wriggly piglets cuddled up with their mother.

"Thank you very much," said James. "It's good to
see Landy working again!"

But Pickup was NOT happy to see Landy.
He revved his engine and roarrrred …
"Get out! This is MY farm now!"

As they drove away, Landy felt very sad to leave all the animals behind.

He didn't beep – not even once.

"Cheer-up Landy," said Jack when they got home.
"We can get some animals and make our own little farm."

"BEEP! BEEP!" said Landy, "I'll be very happy here!"

They made their plans as the sun went down.

That night Landy felt so excited –
he could hardly sleep.